To Jan and Devin

Every night before I go to sleep,
my daddy brings me a glass of water.

Then he reads me a story,
gives me a kiss,

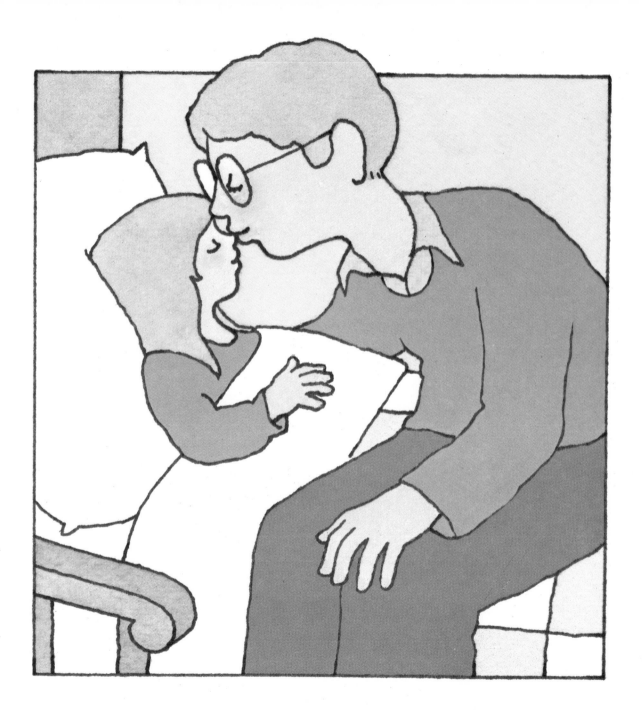

and turns out the light.

But one night before I went to sleep,
I asked my daddy for a horsey ride.

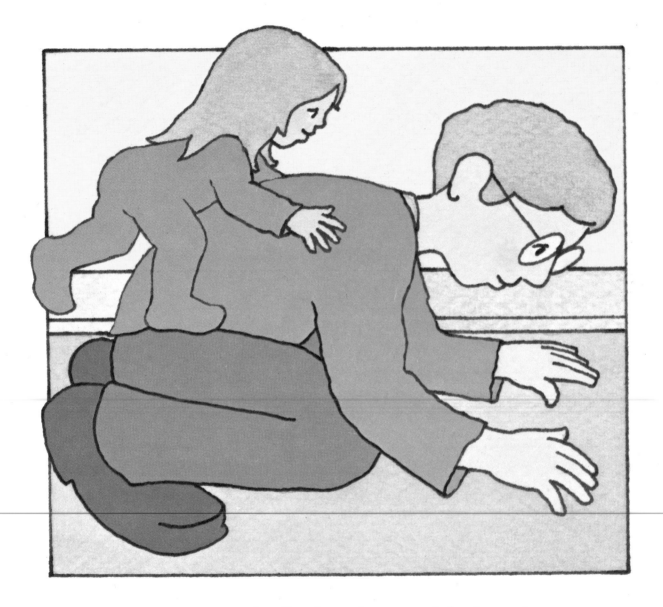

As soon as I climbed onto his back...

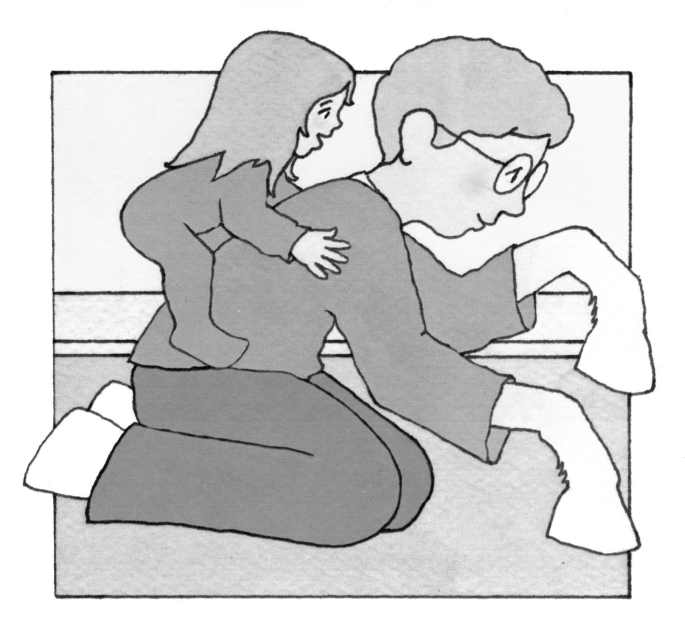

his hands and feet became hooves.

His ears got longer,
and he grew a tail…

just like a real horsey.

And I felt like an Indian princess…

riding through the forest.

"Giddyap," I said, and we galloped

as fast as the wind.

Until the sun went down,
and my horsey said...

"Time for bed."

Then he brought me a glass of water,

read me a story,

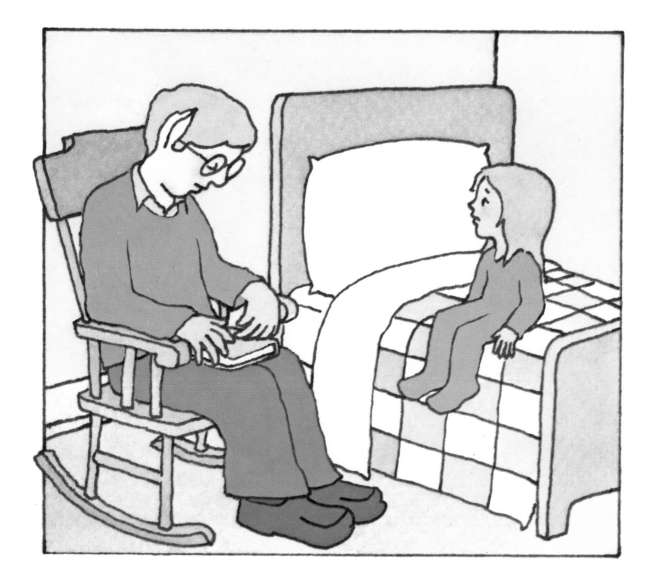

and fell asleep!

"Poor Daddy," I thought.
"He must be very tired."

So I gave him a kiss
and turned out the light.

Goodnight.

Simon and Schuster Books for Young Readers
Simon & Schuster Building
Rockefeller Center
1230 Avenue of the Americas
New York, New York 10020

Published by the Simon & Schuster Juvenile Division
SIMON AND SCHUSTER BOOKS FOR YOUNG READERS
is a trademark of Simon & Schuster Inc.

Manufactured in the United States of America

10 9 8 7 6 5 4 3 2

10 9 8 7 6 5 4 3 2 1 pbk

Library of Congress Cataloging in Publication Data
Asch, Frank. Goodnight horsey.
SUMMARY: A request for a bedtime glass of water results
in a fantastic horsey ride with a surprise ending.
[1. Bedtime—Fiction] I. Title.
PZ7.A778Gp 1981 [E] 81-7332
ISBN 0-671-66277-5 AACR2
ISBN 0-671-66278-3 Pbk

GOODNIGHT HORSEY

FRANK ASCH

A Little Simon Book
Published by Simon & Schuster, Inc.